Javier's Dream

By Linda Sib'

Perfection Learning®

Cover & Inside Illustration: Dea Marks
Designer: Emily J. Greazel

About the Author

Linda Sibley has lived in Harlingen, Texas, her entire life, except for one year away at school. She now lives there with her husband, Rick, and two children, Jeremy and Jennifer.

Ms. Sibley did contract work for attorneys for 15 years so she could be at home to raise her children. Now she is working at a local hospital part-time. This enables her to spend time writing, which is her favorite thing to do. She also enjoys reading and searching for interesting antiques.

Traveling is another of Ms. Sibley's interests. So far she has visited 24 states and 2 countries. She is always looking for an excuse to go on another trip.

For information, contact
Perfection Learning® Corporation
1000 North Second Avenue, P.O. Box 500
Logan, Iowa 51546-0500.
Phone: 1-800-831-4190
Fax: 1-800-543-2745
perfectionlearning.com

PB ISBN-10: 0-7891-5736-5 ISBN-13: 978-0-7891-5736-2
RLB ISBN-10: 0-7569-0926-0 ISBN-13: 978-0-7569-0926-0
5 6 7 8 9 10 PP 13 12 11 10 09 08

Contents

1
The Summer Job

The sun was just beginning to rise. The temperature was already 80 degrees. I wiped my sweaty forehead on my shirtsleeve. It was going to be another long, hot day.

At 7:30 a.m., I was headed for the field. I had already eaten breakfast. I had even helped Joe grease the cotton pickers.

This sure wasn't how I'd planned to spend my summer. But the funny thing was that I was enjoying myself anyway.

We traveled in our usual caravan to the field near the river. I rode in the lead cotton picker with Joe. The second picker was driven by Fausto. Alfonso followed along with the module builder. Gramps brought up the rear in his old Ford truck.

"How many acres are in this field, Joe?" I asked.

"About 100, *mas o menos*, Miguel," he replied.

I hated it when he answered me in Spanish. He always called me Miguel too. That was my name in Spanish. Everyone else called me Michael.

I think he did it just to aggravate me. He knew I didn't understand a word he said. I didn't have any desire to learn Spanish either. That seemed to bug him.

I was going to ask how long it took to pick 100 acres. Joe must have read my mind. He answered before I could ask.

"We'll finish it up tomorrow," he said. "Then we'll move back to the barn. We still have 80 acres to pick over there."

"Why is Gramps' farm all spread out?" I asked.

"Most farmers can't afford to own much of this expensive farmland," he explained. "Your grandfather owns 120 acres near his house. Then he has a farm lease on this 100-acre block by the river."

"Sounds confusing," I said.

"Not really," he continued. "He leases the 100 acres from the landowner. He pays for the seed, chemicals, and irrigation. He also does all the planting and harvesting. Then he splits the profits with the landowner."

It sounded like too much work to me. I started to say so but decided against it.

Joe drove the cotton picker into the field. A sea of white cotton lay before us.

"Señor Dawson has a good crop this year," Joe said. "We'll probably pick a bale and a half to the acre."

I knew Joe's estimate would be correct. After all, he had worked for Gramps for over 30 years.

Gramps said Joe was born in Tampico, Mexico. His family was very poor. Joe was the oldest of eight children. That meant it was his responsibility to help support his family.

So Joe had crossed the Rio Grande when he was barely 15. He'd been looking for work, and Gramps had offered him a job. Joe said Gramps had treated him right since that first day. He had no reason to look further.

Joe lined up the picker with the first two rows. I watched as cotton began feeding into the picker. Then I checked the side mirrors. Only the naked plant was left behind. The fluffy white cotton was blown into the basket behind us.

Fausto started picking a few rows over. Alfonso positioned the module builder on the turn row. Gramps parked behind the module builder. He watched from his air-conditioned pickup.

I noticed he stayed in his truck a lot this summer. His heart attack in the spring had really worried him. He was doing his best to follow his doctor's advice. Still, he insisted he had to get his cotton picked. That's why Dad had proposed the idea of a summer job.

"You could work for your grandfather this summer," Dad had suggested. "You could make pretty good money. And I'd feel better if you looked after him.

"Gran tries to slow him down," he continued. "But he doesn't always listen to her."

The idea of working for Gramps felt strange. I really wasn't that close to my grandparents. We mainly saw one another on holidays.

The thought of making money appealed to me though. But then I remembered all the things I'd miss out on.

"It sounds like a good idea," I lied. "But there's no way I can go."

Dad raised one eyebrow. "Why's that?" he asked.

"Grady and I have plans," I said. "We're going to baseball camp for two weeks."

"We can work that out," Dad said.

"There are other reasons too," I said. "You wanted me to keep the pool clean all summer. And Mom wants me to clean out the garage."

"We'll just hire someone to take care of the pool," Dad said. "And the garage can wait."

I struggled to think of something good. Something *so* good, he'd change his mind.

I didn't want to give up my summer freedom. I'd endured nine long months of school. I was looking forward to kicking back a little. My plans included sleeping late, spending time in the pool, and hanging out with my best friend, Grady.

But Dad had already made up his mind. I could tell by the look on his face. Even Mom agreed that it was a good idea.

They said I could at least help harvest the cotton. They promised to fly me home before baseball camp. And that was the end of the discussion.

Before I knew it, I was on my way to Santa Maria, Texas—population 210. It was the last place I thought I'd spend my summer.

I watched as Joe reached the end of the row. He turned the picker expertly. Then he lined it up with two more rows.

"Do you know what river that is?" Joe asked. He pointed to the water running along the south side of the field.

"Nope," I answered without much interest.

I didn't have any idea where I was. It was impossible to tell. Cotton fields spread out in every direction.

"That's the Rio Grande," he said. "Do you see the land on the other side?"

9

"Yeah," I said, still uninterested.

"That's Mexico," he pointed out.

"You're kidding!" I said. "I didn't know Gramps farmed this close to Mexico."

"Sure he does," Joe said. "Their house is just four miles north of the river."

"I'd like to walk down to the river," I said eagerly. "Just to take a look around."

"You'll stay away if you know what's good for you," Joe said sharply. "There's all kinds of trouble to get into."

"What do you mean?" I asked in surprise.

"It's different when you work along the river." Joe frowned. "You have to mind your own business."

Then he mumbled a little in Spanish and English. I only caught two words. They sounded like "runners" and "coyotes."

I knew better than to ask more questions. He would probably answer me in Spanish anyway.

I studied the river and the land on both sides. It looked so peaceful. What kind of trouble could I possibly get into?

Joe didn't say a word after that. He was hard to figure out sometimes. I got the feeling he didn't like me much. He seemed to think I was a spoiled rich kid.

I thought back to my arrival the week before. Joe hadn't wasted any time putting me to work. My first job had been to help get the pickers ready.

Joe had slapped a grease gun in my hand. He told me to grease every part that moved. I'd never had any training with a grease gun before.

By the end of the day, I was a mess. A glob of grease sat on top of each boot. Several big smears ran down each pant leg. My hands were covered with the thick black goo. That gave the guys something to laugh about.

"We can tell you're a city boy," they chuckled. "There's more grease on you than both pickers put together."

Their teasing didn't bother me a bit. But I was worried about what Gran would say. Before I went in the house, I scrubbed my hands and face. I tried to wipe the excess off my clothes. But all I did was smear it in a little deeper.

But Gran didn't throw a fit about washing my clothes. In fact, she burst out laughing when she saw me. She said she'd washed clothes that looked a lot worse.

Now, riding with Joe was getting boring—especially since he wasn't going to talk anymore. When he stopped to empty the basket, I climbed down. I decided to sit in the truck with Gramps.

"Joe says you have a good crop this year," I said to Gramps.

"It sure looks that way." He smiled. "The price looks good this year too. I just want to get the cotton picked and out of the field as soon as possible."

11

"What's the hurry?" I asked. "You have all summer."

"That's what I thought back in '72," Gramps said. "I had 400 acres of cotton that summer. I'd only been picking for a couple of days. Then a hailstorm came through. It wiped out nearly the whole crop. You never know what Mother Nature has in mind."

"Aren't you ready to quit farming?" I asked then. "It seems like so much hard work."

"It *is* a lot of hard work," Gramps agreed. "But I have farming in my blood. It's not something I can just walk away from.

"Besides," he added. "I have good men working for me. That makes a big difference. Fausto and Alfonso have been here over 15 years. Joe's been here since your dad was about your size."

It was funny to hear him say that. I couldn't believe Dad was ever my size. I sure couldn't picture him with grease up to his elbows. And I definitely couldn't imagine him driving tractors.

Dad was always perfectly groomed. It didn't matter what time of day it was. He wore suits and ties to work every day. Even on the weekends, he never lay around in shorts and old T-shirts. He always looked ready to go somewhere important.

"Why didn't Dad go into farming with you?" I asked. I couldn't remember if Dad and I had ever talked about it.

"Your dad had his own dreams," said Gramps. "Ever since he could hold a pencil, he loved to draw. He'd take a plain piece of paper and use his imagination. He'd draw some amazing designs. It seemed natural that he become an architect."

Gramps was right. Dad *could* design and draw anything. His new firm was in demand all over the country.

Dad had already tried to interest me in drafting. He'd even bought me a drafting table for Christmas. But I hadn't figured out what I wanted to do yet. I was pretty sure, though, that I didn't want to be an architect.

We watched Fausto dump a basket of cotton into the module builder. Then we walked over to watch Alfonso operate the machine. I climbed the metal ladder and stood on the platform to watch. He worked the controls easily.

The module builder compacted the loose cotton into a giant rectangle—a module. It was hard to believe that one module was equal to twelve regular-size cotton bales. Once the module was built, it was dropped on the turn row.

Then came my favorite part. I painted a big number on the end with black spray paint. That was followed by the initials MD. They identified the module for the cotton gin.

After the module was marked, a module-hauling truck arrived. It picked up the module and delivered it to the gin. The gin workers saw the initials. Then they knew it was from Michael Dawson Farms.

A few minutes before noon, I saw a trail of dust. It was rising above the gravel road in the distance. That was always a welcome sign. It meant Gran was on the way with lunch.

We didn't go home for lunch during cotton harvesting. Gramps didn't want to waste the daylight hours. So we stopped working just long enough to eat.

I was thrilled to see Gran had brought my favorite—fried chicken. She made the best fried chicken on earth. She had cole slaw and mashed potatoes too.

But the best thing of all was the iced tea. Summer days in South Texas were plenty hot. Gran always brought a big thermos with extra sugar just for me.

Before long, the trail of dust was headed the other direction. Gran was on her way back home again.

After lunch, Gramps and I went to the gin. He liked to watch his cotton being ginned.

Later we went to the barn and hooked up to the diesel tank. He had it fixed so he could pull it to the field with his truck. I even helped him fill the tractor and pickers with diesel. The drivers had time for a quick break. Then they went right back to work with a full tank of fuel.

I stayed busy, and the afternoon passed quickly. It was dark when we made it back to the house.

"Are you boys hungry?" Gran called from the kitchen.

"Starving!" I called back. I had never been so hungry in all my life. But then, I had never worked so hard in all my life either.

"It's picking pretty well," Gramps said. "We're getting a bale and a half per acre."

I smiled when I remembered Joe's estimate. His guess had been exactly right.

"We ought to be finished there tomorrow," Gramps said. Then he paused for a minute and looked at me.

"How do you feel about driving a tractor?" he asked.

I stopped chewing and stared at him in surprise. "Me?" I asked.

"You can drive the 7400 John Deere," he said. "Someone needs to start shredding cotton stalks. You seem to be a responsible young man."

I smiled and sat up a little taller in my chair.

"Great," I said excitedly. "I'm sure I can do that."

Immediately I wondered why I'd said that. I wasn't at all sure I could do that. I didn't know anything about driving a tractor.

"It'll probably take three days to shred the hundred acres," Gramps said thoughtfully. "Then you can shred the 40 acres we've already picked."

"Okay," I said. "I'd be glad to."

"Now, Dawson," Gran said. "I don't know if that would be a good idea."

(Gran always called Gramps by his last name. I thought it was kind of cool.)

"He's new at this," she said. "I don't think you should leave him in the field alone."

I didn't realize I was going to be left alone. That didn't sound like a good idea to me either.

"I won't leave him alone," Gramps said.

I felt better and grinned happily.

"At least not on the first day," he added.

I stopped grinning.

"I'll tell you what," Gramps said. "We'll take the tractor to the field in the morning. You can shred for a while. We'll see how you do."

"Okay," I said.

Part of me was excited about driving a tractor. Grady was going to be really impressed. But the other half of me was nervous. What if I lost control and ended up in the river?

I reassured myself that I would be all right. After all, I was a good swimmer.

2

Driving Lessons

The next morning, Gramps got me out of bed at 5:30. Before I finished eating, he was ready to go out to the field. The screen door banged behind me as I followed him out the back door. I was still buttoning my shirt. A biscuit hung out of my mouth.

Gramps walked straight to the barn. He stopped between his truck and the tractor.

"Which one do you want to drive to the field?" he asked.

"Are you kidding me?" I asked in disbelief. "I don't know how to drive. I don't have a driver's license yet."

"Your dad drove on the farm by the time he was 12," Gramps said.

"He did?" I asked in surprise.

Gramps stood there shaking his head. "You mean you've never been behind the wheel before?"

"Gramps!" I said. "My parents would never let me drive. I'm not old enough."

"Well, you're going to have to be old enough today," he said. "Have you at least *watched* your dad drive?"

"Of course," I said. "I know the basics of driving. I've just never actually done it."

"Well, you can drive the truck," Gramps decided. "Drive real slow, and follow me to the field."

I looked at him in shock. I couldn't believe he was serious.

"You'll be safe enough on these old roads," Gramps said.

He climbed onto the tractor and started the engine. I climbed into the truck and hoped I could start the engine.

The key was already in the ignition. When I turned it, the old truck jumped to life. I smiled and relaxed. This was going to be a cinch.

I studied the gear shift and began to get nervous again. I had forgotten what all the letters stood for.

The P was for *park*, and the D was for *drive*. The R was for something . . . something that I couldn't remember. I had no idea what the N was for. Hopefully I wouldn't need R and N.

I put my foot on the brake. Then I started to shift out of park. When I did, my foot slipped off the brake. The truck started going backwards!

I stomped down on the brake pedal. That sent me flying forward in the seat. My head almost banged against the steering wheel. I could see Gramps in the tractor. He was laughing at me.

I finally managed to shift into drive. I gripped the steering wheel with both hands. Then I carefully pushed down on the gas pedal. Somehow I managed to follow the tractor.

Gramps puttered along at 25 miles an hour. Even at that speed, I struggled to keep the truck on the road. Thank goodness there wasn't any traffic. If I ran off the road, I'd only end up in a field.

We made it to his field without a problem. Joe and Fausto were already running the pickers. I honked the horn to make sure they realized I was driving the truck.

Gramps climbed down off the tractor. He motioned for me to get behind the wheel.

"You did a good job," he said, smiling. "Let's see what you can do with this one."

I climbed into the cab of the tractor and adjusted the mirrors. Then I made sure the air conditioner vents were blowing on me. I wondered how people had survived the summer heat before air-conditioning was invented.

"Here are the gears," Gramps said loudly over the roar of the motor. "First, second, and third are here. Push in your clutch over there when you shift gears.

"And that's your brake," Gramps pointed out and laughed. "You might want to know where that is."

He rode with me for a couple of rounds. Finally he was satisfied I could handle the tractor. He went back to his truck and watched from there.

I was feeling pretty cool driving that tractor. Grady would never believe it. In one day, I'd driven a pickup *and* a tractor.

My excitement lasted about an hour. Then it began to wear off. All I saw were long, boring rows of cotton stalks.

I hummed for a while. I even sang our school fight song.

Our fight song was one of my favorite things. We sang it before our baseball games. Everyone in the stands stood up and joined in. It gave me chills every time.

I was singing the chorus for the third time when I saw a movement by the river. I stared hard at the brush. Whatever it was disappeared in the mesquite trees. I kept watching, and before long, I saw it again.

It was a man! He was running along the American side of the river. He was running hard—as if his life depended on it.

I watched as he dodged in and out of the brush. He kept looking back over his shoulder.

Then I saw a green and white Suburban. It was racing along the river too. It seemed to be chasing the man.

I stopped the tractor in the middle of the field to watch.

The Suburban quickly caught up with the man. Two men dressed in green uniforms jumped out. They grabbed the man and put him inside. Then they drove away.

I could hardly believe what had happened. I had obviously just witnessed a kidnapping! I needed to get some help.

Joe and Fausto were at the other end of the field. Gramps was with them. I had to let them know what had happened. They needed to call the police.

I drove the tractor to the edge of the field. I shut it off and jumped out of the cab. I ran as hard as I could to Gramps' truck.

"Did you see that?" I asked out of breath. "Two men just kidnapped a guy!"

"What are you talking about?" Gramps asked in surprise.

"Didn't you see those men?" I asked. "They were driving a green and white Suburban. They grabbed a man along the river. Then they put him inside the van and took off."

"The man wasn't kidnapped," Gramps said patiently. "That was the border patrol."

"What's the border patrol?" I asked.

"People who patrol the border," he said. He spoke as if he were explaining it to a little child. "They arrest people who cross the border illegally."

"Why?" I asked.

"So they can return them to Mexico," Gramps explained.

"But what if the people want to stay in the United States?" I asked. "Maybe they don't want to go back to Mexico."

"I'll explain it to you later, Michael," Gramps said. Now his voice sounded angry. "You're wasting daylight hours. You need to get back to work."

"Okay," I said. I turned away and kicked clods of dirt as I walked. I hated it when people talked to me that way.

I may not know anything about the border patrol, but I did know what I'd seen. And it had sure looked like a kidnapping!

3
A Game of Catch

I shredded cotton stalks all afternoon. I thought of a lot of questions to ask Gramps. But I never got the chance that night. It was late when we got home. We ate some cold fried chicken and went to bed.

The next morning, Gramps drove me back to the field. Everyone else moved to the 80 acres by the house. On the way, we had a few minutes to talk.

"You might see the border patrol by the river again," Gramps said. "But don't worry about it. They're just doing their job."

"Okay," I said.

"Just stay in the tractor, and get your shredding done," he ordered. "It's not always safe down by the river."

That was the second time I'd been told that. I couldn't see what the big deal was. It was just a boring little river.

Gramps waited for me to get the tractor started. Then he left for the other field. Every couple of hours, he came back to check on me. He brought my lunch at noon. Another time, he brought me iced tea and a candy bar.

Meanwhile, I kept a close eye on the river. The green and white Suburban returned before lunch. It traveled slowly along the river and then disappeared.

Nothing else stirred. Not even the patch of white across the river moved. I'd been watching it all day. I couldn't figure out what it was.

My shredding took me closer and closer to the river. Finally, my curiosity got the best of me. I stopped the tractor and climbed down. After all, the river looked perfectly safe to me.

I made my way through the brush and overgrown grass. I walked right to the water's edge. I couldn't believe I was only 100 feet from Mexico!

My eyes searched the other side of the river. They fell on that familiar white patch. Now I was close enough to see what it was. It was a white shirt worn by a Mexican boy. He'd been sitting there watching me all this time.

It felt kind of weird. Should I wave or just ignore him? Finally, I decided to speak and see what happened.

"Hello!" I yelled. I waved my arms high above my head.

He seemed to hesitate for a moment. Then he waved silently in return.

"What are you doing?" I shouted.

He stood up and waved again. But he still didn't speak. Then I realized he probably couldn't speak English.

My curiosity kept growing. Why had he been sitting there all day watching me work? For the first time, I wished I could speak Spanish.

We stood there staring at each other. We had no way to communicate. Then I had an idea. I turned and ran back to the tractor.

My baseball was under the seat. I had tossed it in there the day before. I had hoped somebody would practice pitching with me during lunch.

I walked as close to the water as possible. It was a pretty long throw across the river.

I hesitated for a minute. Losing my baseball in the brush wouldn't make me happy. Even worse, it might fall short and land in the river.

Javier's Dream

I decided to take a chance. Using all my strength, I threw the ball toward the boy. It fell about three feet in front of him.

I watched as he picked up the ball and inspected it. He examined it for a long time. I was beginning to worry. Maybe he didn't understand he was supposed to throw it back. Maybe I would lose my ball after all.

But eventually he did throw it back. I was impressed. He had a really good arm.

We started throwing the baseball back and forth. It was amazing when I thought about it. We were playing catch between two countries.

The boy seemed to be having a great time. Sometimes the wind blew just right. It carried the sound of his laughter across the river.

One time, I didn't throw the baseball back. Instead, I stopped and pointed to myself.

"My name is Michael!" I shouted. "Michael!"

He hesitated only a minute. Then he smiled and shouted, "*Yo soy Javier!*"

I was so proud. We were actually communicating now.

"Javier!" I shouted as I threw the ball back in a wide arc.

"Miguel!" he shouted when he returned the throw.

I don't know how long we played catch. But I totally forgot about tractors and cotton stalks—until I turned around to get the ball and saw that familiar trail of dust. Gramps was on his way to the field.

I remembered his warning. He'd said to stay away from the river. I also knew that I'd goofed off way too long.

I yelled good-bye to Javier and started running. Gramps pulled up as I was climbing into the tractor.

He stepped out of his truck with a frown. "Is something wrong with the tractor?" he asked.

"I just needed to stretch my legs," I lied.

"Don't be stretching your legs this close to the river," he warned.

"Okay," I said. It didn't seem like a good time to tell him about Javier. I decided to keep it a secret for a while.

"Let's go back to the house now," Gramps said. "I'm tired and ready to call it a day."

"But I didn't finish the field yet," I said.

"That's all right," he said. "You can finish it tomorrow."

"Are you feeling all right?" I asked him.

"Just tired," he repeated. "Why don't you drive for me?"

"Okay," I said. I was always happy to have another chance to drive.

During dinner, we had a long talk about the river. I wanted to know all about the border patrol. I also wanted to know why the river was dangerous.

Gran and Gramps explained everything. Gramps said the border patrol was part of the Immigration and Naturalization Service. That was part of the Department of Justice. It was the border patrol's job to watch almost 2,000 miles of border. They returned illegal immigrants to Mexico. They also arrested drug traffickers and illegal-immigrant smugglers.

It was illegal for Mexican citizens to cross the river. They had to enter the United States at a legal port of entry, like the International Bridge at Brownsville. There they had to pass through customs with a visa and pay a fee.

"Then why don't they all enter the right way?" I asked.

"Only a set number of people can enter the United States each year," Gran said. "And they need a visa. The people who cross the river are poor. They can't get visas and pay the fees. That's the whole reason they come here. They want to find jobs that will pay better wages."

"I still don't see what's so dangerous," I said.

"Some people who cross the river are criminals," Gramps said. "They use the river to transport illegal drugs. I read a story in the newspaper just this week. The border patrol arrested four men. They were floating 1,500 pounds of marijuana across the river on a raft."

"Drug traffickers are dangerous people," Gran added. "They would do just about anything to get their drugs across the river."

"Then you also have the coyotes," Gramps said.

"And he doesn't mean wild dogs," Gran explained. "Coyotes are the worst kind of smugglers. They smuggle illegal immigrants into the United States."

"Why is that so bad?" I asked. "It sounds like they're just trying to help."

"First, they're breaking the law," Gramps said. "Second, coyotes have no concern for the immigrants. All they really want is money. They charge the immigrants to smuggle them into the United States.

"I can tell you stories that would cause your hair to stand on end," he added.

I had to ask. "What kind of stories?"

"Coyotes have been known to pack 100 illegal immigrants into a train car. They're locked in there for several days without food or water.

"Sometimes they lock them in semitrailers going north. There's no ventilation in those trailers, so many of them die. Hundreds of people have lost their lives because of coyotes."

I was definitely beginning to see the dangers. Drug smugglers and coyotes made the Rio Grande a lot less inviting. But I still wasn't satisfied. I had a lot of questions left.

"Why do people need coyotes?" I asked. "They could just swim across on their own. It's not very far."

"It's an unusual river," Gramps said. "There are places where it's shallow. A person can wade across. But the border patrol guards those areas heavily.

"In other places, the water doesn't look deep. But it can fool you. You can start out in water that's only five feet deep. Then suddenly it drops to 20 feet."

"There are whirlpools in the river too," Gran pointed out. "If you get caught in one, it will pull you under."

"A strong current runs underneath the surface," Gramps said. "Even strong swimmers have been known to drown."

"Then why don't they come across in boats?" I asked.

Gramps seemed to be getting a little annoyed now. But he answered anyway.

"They do try to cross in rafts and boats," he explained. "Sometimes they make it across. But most of the time, the border patrol spots them. Lots of times their rickety boats don't make it. The immigrants get dumped into the river and have to battle the current."

"I still don't think it looks all that hard," I argued. "I also don't understand why the U.S. doesn't let them come here."

"Well, you don't need to understand it!" Gramps barked. "Just stay away from the river like I told you to!"

"Dawson!" Gran scolded him.

"I'm sorry," Gramps said. He sighed deeply. "It's been a long day. I think I'll go to bed."

Gran and I watched in silence as he left the room.

"He's not feeling well," she said softly. "He doesn't mean to sound so harsh, Michael."

I didn't know what to say, so I excused myself and went outside.

I searched the barn for the guys. Fausto and Joe still hadn't come in from picking. But Alfonso was in the barn working on a trailer.

"*Como esta?*" he asked.

I surprised myself by answering, "*Bien.*" At least I'd learned to say "good" in Spanish.

"No more work today?" Alfonso asked.

"No," I said as I leaned against the trailer. "Gramps didn't feel well. He wanted to come in early."

I watched Alfonso as he worked. It was hard not to notice his hands. They were rough and calloused from years of hard work. Dirt was buried deep around his fingernails. It didn't look as if it could ever be scrubbed out.

"Alfonso," I asked. "Were you born in Mexico?"

"In Tamaulipas, Mexico," he said with a thick accent.

"Did you come to the United States to work?" I asked.

"*Sí,*" he said. "I did."

"How did you get here?" I pressed.

He stopped working and looked at me.

"I crossed the river at night with a friend," he said. "It was many years ago. Señor Dawson gave me a job and a home here. So I got my papers from the government. Now I'm a legal resident of the United States."

"Do you ever go back to visit?" I asked.

"Sí." He smiled. "I visit my family in Tamaulipas. I go in the winter when there is no work."

I watched quietly as he continued working.

"Do you like living in Dallas?" he asked me.

"Yeah, it's okay," I said.

"You have many friends there?" he asked.

"Yeah, a few," I answered.

"And your *novia*?" he asked and smiled again.

"What's a *novia*?" I had to ask.

"A girlfriend," he explained.

"No." I grinned. "I don't have a girlfriend. They're too much trouble."

Alfonso laughed loudly and nodded his head. "You are very smart for a young man," he said.

Alfonso seemed like someone I could trust. So I told him how Javier had watched me all day.

"Why did he just sit there watching me?" I asked.

"He does what I did as a boy," Alfonso said sadly. "He looks at the other side of the river and dreams."

"What do you mean?" I asked.

"He dreams of living in the United States someday," he explained.

"But all he has to do is cross the river," I said. "It looks like it would be so easy."

"But what would he do?" asked Alfonso. "He has no family—no one to care for him. And crossing the river is not as easy as it looks."

"But you and your friend did it," I reminded him.

"Yes, *I* made it across the river," he said slowly. "But my friend did not. He got tired and could not swim all the way."

I hated to ask, but I had to. "What happened to him?" I asked.

"*Muerto*," Alfonso said. "He's dead."

I was sorry I'd brought up the story about Javier. "I'm sorry," I said.

"It was many years ago," he said.

"I want to write a letter to Javier in Spanish," I told Alfonso after a moment of silence. "Can you help me?"

"But I cannot read and write," Alfonso pointed out.

"Just tell me the words and I'll write them," I said. "I'll get an English-Spanish dictionary to help us."

"I will try," he said. "But why do you want to write him a letter?"

"I'm not sure," I answered honestly.

I didn't know how to explain it to him. It seemed silly even to me. How could I feel such a strong urge to help Javier? I didn't even know him. All we had done was play catch across the Rio Grande for a little while.

4
Special Delivery

I dashed into the house and grabbed some paper and a pen. Gran said I could borrow her dictionary. She looked at me strangely but didn't ask why I wanted it. I was relieved. I didn't want to tell her what I was doing. But I didn't want to lie to her either.

Alfonso was waiting for me in the barn. I told him what I wanted the letter to say. Then he told me how to say it in Spanish. With his help and the dictionary, I was able to write a letter.

The letter was very simple. I explained that I was visiting my grandparents. I told Javier I was helping my grandfather harvest his cotton crop. We were finishing the letter when Joe walked into the barn.

"What are you two up to?" Joe asked.

I didn't want Joe to know anything about Javier. I looked at Alfonso for help.

"I'm helping Michael learn Spanish," Alfonso said. "And he's helping me learn English."

"But Miguel does not wish to learn Spanish," Joe said with a frown.

The two of them began speaking Spanish. It was a good time to escape to the house.

I folded the letter carefully and put it in my jeans pocket. After a shower, I watched TV with Gran for a while. At bedtime, I was still wide awake.

I lay in bed staring at the ceiling. I kept picturing Javier watching me from across the river. I was anxious to get back to the field the next morning.

"Maybe Alfonso should finish shredding," Gramps said at breakfast.

Oh, no! That would ruin everything.

"I feel bad about leaving you by the river alone," he said.

"But I don't mind," I assured him. "I'll probably finish it up today anyway."

"Are you sure you don't mind?" Gramps asked.

"No," I said. "I really want to do it."

He agreed and I was relieved. I had almost missed my chance to see Javier.

After breakfast, Gramps dropped me off at the field. I'd made three rounds when I saw Javier. He was sitting in the same spot as the day before.

I stopped the tractor at the edge of the field. I climbed down and took the note from my pocket. I wrapped it tightly around the baseball. Then I used a rubber band to hold it in place. I hurried to the river's edge.

Javier stood up and yelled, "Miguel!"

"Hi, Javier!" I shouted. I threw the ball in a wide arc. Javier caught it.

I watched as he examined the ball. He pulled the paper off and opened it. He studied it for a few minutes and then waved again. Without another word, he turned and ran away. He took the note and my baseball with him.

I was confused. Where was he going? My baseball was gone—and I didn't get an answer to my letter.

There was nothing I could do about it now. I decided to go back to work. Every time I finished a row, I looked to see if he had returned. There wasn't a sign of him anywhere.

At lunch, Gramps showed up with a roast beef sandwich. He sat and talked to me while I ate.

"You should be finished in a couple more hours," he observed.

My mouth was too full to answer. "Mm-hmm," I said.

"Then I can move you to the 40 acres east of the house," he said. "You can shred that too if you want to."

"That's okay with me," I said.

He was quiet, so I continued eating. But I could tell something was on his mind.

"Michael," he said. "I'm sorry about snapping at you last night. I didn't feel well, but that was no excuse."

"It's okay, Gramps," I said.

"No, it's not okay," he said. "I don't expect a young man like you to understand. But it's hard when your body starts wearing out. I still want to do the things I did when I was your age. But my tired, old body just can't keep up."

I wanted to say something to make him feel better. But I couldn't think of anything.

He stood up slowly to leave. "I'll be back in a couple of hours," he said. "Then we can move you to the other field. Or if you're tired, you can leave the rest until tomorrow."

"Okay," I agreed.

I watched his old Ford truck disappear. It was hard for me to understand how he felt. I thought being 20 was old. I couldn't imagine being Gramps' age. But I couldn't help feeling sorry for him either.

I was making the last round when I noticed Javier. He was waving his arms above his head. Quickly, I parked the tractor and ran to the water's edge.

Javier had the baseball in his hand. He called my name and threw it across the river. As soon as I caught it, I felt the paper.

I pulled off the rubber band and unfolded the paper. It was a different letter. This one was from him.

Most of the letter was written in English. There was a short passage in Spanish at the end. I read the English part.

Javier had two brothers and three sisters. The sisters lived with his mother in Veracruz. His brother Sergio lived in Cancún. He worked for a big hotel there.

His other brother, Ignacio, worked in a *maquiladora* plant in Nuevo Progresso. Alfonso told me later that a maquiladora plant was a factory in Mexico owned by a large U.S. company.

Ignacio was learning English. He could write a little in English, so he'd helped Javier write the letter.

Javier's mother couldn't care for Javier, so she let him live with Ignacio. Javier was bored when his brother was working. That's why he came to the river.

The rest of the letter was written in Spanish. I would need the dictionary or Alfonso's help to read it.

I needed to explain to Javier that I was moving to another field. Only I didn't know how to tell him. Then I saw the dust rising and knew Gramps was returning.

"I have to go!" I yelled at Javier. "Good-bye!"

He waved again with a big smile. I had no choice but to hurry back to the tractor. I was waiting there when Gramps arrived.

"Everything all right?" he called from the truck.

"Yes, sir," I answered.

"Okay, then," he said. "Just follow me."

I turned to look at the river one more time. I couldn't see Javier. I wondered if I would ever see him again.

5
The Warning

Gramps led me to the 40-acre field. I parked the tractor on the turn row. Then we agreed to call it a day. The stalks would have to wait until tomorrow.

Gramps was talkative on the ride home. I was glad he seemed to be feeling better. I asked what time Alfonso would be coming in. He said it would probably be late. It looked as if I'd have to figure out the Spanish words myself.

Gramps rested while Gran cooked dinner. That gave me a chance to work on the letter. I got the dictionary and went right to work.

It was like putting together pieces of a puzzle. I looked up one word at a time. Slowly the message began to make sense. When I finished, I was shocked.

My brother does not know this, but I have a plan. I am going to the United States. I will cross the river soon. Silently I read the words to myself again.

It sounded as if Javier planned to cross the river alone. Didn't he know about the dangers? Somehow I had to warn him.

I stuck the letter deep into my pocket. After dinner, I went to the barn to wait for Alfonso. It was after dark when he arrived.

"Alfonso," I whispered. "We need to talk."

He grabbed a flashlight and followed me outside. He held the flashlight while I read the letter to him. When I finished, he was upset.

"He should not try to cross the river alone," Alfonso said. "It is much too dangerous for a boy on his own."

"How can I warn him?" I asked.

"We will write another letter," he said. "We will tell him not to try to cross the river."

"But how will I get the letter to him?" I asked. "I won't be there tomorrow. Gramps moved me to another field."

"We will find a way," Alfonso said.

We waited until Joe and Fausto went to bed. Then we sat under the dim light in the barn. We worked on the letter for over an hour.

Alfonso told me to write *PELIGRO* in capital letters at the top of the letter. It meant "danger." We explained about the deep water, fast currents, and whirlpools. We warned him about the border patrol. Finally, we told him about drug dealers on the river.

When we finished, I put the letter in my pocket. I was still worried about delivering it.

When I walked into the house, Gran was talking on the phone. "I was just going to come looking for you," she said to me. "Your parents want to say hello. They're on the speakerphone. You can talk to both of them."

"Hi, Mom," I said. "Hi, Dad."

"Hi," they said in unison. "How are you?"

"I'm fine," I said. "I've been driving the tractor for Gramps."

"That's what we hear," Dad said. "I heard you even drove his pickup."

"Yep," I said proudly. "I drove it all the way out to the field."

"Gramps said you're doing a good job," Dad said. "We're proud of you for helping out so much."

"Is everything going okay?" Mom asked.

I hesitated for a minute. I really wanted to tell them about Javier. But I knew I couldn't. They would forbid me to go anywhere near the river. Then I wouldn't be able to warn Javier.

"Everything is fine," I fibbed.

They caught me up on the news at home. They passed on a hello from Grady. I reminded them to tell Grady I had driven a truck and a tractor.

"Well," Mom said finally, "we'll let you get ready for bed. I'm sure you're tired."

"Yeah," I agreed. "Gramps works me pretty hard." I said that just loud enough for Gramps to hear. He chuckled.

My sleep was full of unsettling dreams that night. I dreamed a coyote was bringing Javier across the river. In the deep waters, the coyote took Javier's money and left him to drown. Javier couldn't swim, and he was calling out to me for help. I was glad when morning came.

After breakfast, we met the others at the barn. Gramps gave them instructions for the day.

"I'll run Michael to the tractor quickly," he told Joe. "Then I'm coming back to the house. Mrs. Dawson and I are going to town. I have a doctor's appointment."

"Señor Dawson," Alfonso said. "I can take Michael to the tractor."

"That would really help me out," Gramps said. "You don't mind?"

"I will be happy to drive him," Alfonso assured Gramps.

I barely gave him a chance to get into the truck. "This is great," I said excitedly. "Now we can get the letter to Javier."

"We will try," Alfonso said. "But we will have to hurry."

Alfonso flew down the road at 60 miles an hour. I clutched the armrest tightly but didn't say a word. A huge cloud of dust filled the air behind us. Gravel flew in every direction.

He drove us close to the river's edge. I scanned the riverbanks for Javier. My heart sank when I realized he wasn't there.

I paced back and forth along the water's edge. What if he had tried to cross the night before? My warning might have come too late.

"We can't wait any longer," Alfonso said. "I have to take you to the field. The others will be waiting for me."

I stared at the baseball in my hand. The letter was wrapped around it securely. The only thing I could do was throw it across the river. Hopefully Javier would find it before it was too late.

A mesquite tree worked as a target. I aimed and threw the ball across the river. It was a direct hit. The ball bounced once and came to rest in a clearing. It wouldn't be hard for Javier to find—if he was looking for it.

Alfonso took me to the tractor. I looked out over the field of cotton stalks. Driving the tractor had lost its excitement—especially since I couldn't watch the river anymore.

Gramps returned from his doctor's visit in a cheerful mood. The doctor had given him a good report. He was also happy about the cotton crop. The last of it would be picked by sundown.

He even took me out for lunch to celebrate. I was glad the doctor had said Gramps was doing well. I was even more thrilled to get out of that cotton field.

We went to El Taquito, Gramps' favorite place. He said they made the best tacos and enchiladas in town. He was definitely right.

Some of his farming buddies were there. We all sat together at a big table. They had fun teasing me about being a city kid. I had never seen Gramps laugh so much.

At the table next to us were three border-patrol agents. I couldn't help staring at them. Their green uniforms looked sharp. A thick black belt held their revolver and handcuffs. A shiny gold-and-blue enamel badge was pinned above the pocket on the left side of their shirts. They looked like nice guys. It was hard to imagine Javier lived in fear of them.

Two hours passed before Gramps dropped me off at the field.

"Do you think you can find your way back to the barn?" Gramps asked.

"Sure," I said. "At first I thought all the cotton fields looked the same. But I know my way around now."

"You're pretty smart for a city kid." He grinned. "I'll be expecting you at the barn before dark."

"Okay," I said.

I put some extra pressure on the gas pedal. I was hoping to finish well before dark. Then I'd have time to make a detour to the river.

When I finished shredding, I headed straight for the river. It was less than four miles away. I was sure I could make it there and back before dark.

I swung out onto the road. Then I pushed the gas pedal to the floor. My mind was focused on Javier. I never even heard the thunder rumbling in the east.

6
A Daring Quest

By the time I reached the river, the sky was darkening. In the distance, I could see streaks of lightning. I realized it might be hard to make it back to the barn before dark.

I drove the tractor close to the river and jumped down. I scanned the other side as I paced. Javier was nowhere in sight.

I walked to the place where I had stood to throw the ball. I studied the area around the tree I'd used as a target. The ball was lying in the same place. Javier had never seen the note!

I had tried so hard to help him. I could only hope he would eventually find the letter.

As I turned to leave, I thought I saw movement in the brush. I turned back and saw Javier. He waved his arms silently in the air.

"Javier!" I shouted with relief.

He didn't shout a greeting in return. Instead, he held his hand to his mouth. He was motioning for me to be quiet.

I shrugged my shoulders and held out my hands in a silent question. He didn't answer. Turning his back to me, he began struggling with something hidden in the brush.

Lightning flashed in the sky. I began to feel uneasy. A big drop of rain hit me on the head. I must have jumped a foot.

A steady rain began to fall. I thought about running to the tractor. I wondered if I should head for home. But what about Javier?

He was still struggling with something. Finally, he pulled it free of the brush. I got a look at it when he reached the water's edge. It was a small canoe! He was going to try to cross the river!

"No!" I screamed. "Go back, Javier!"

He ignored my cries. He climbed into the canoe and shoved away from the Mexican soil.

I held my breath as he started paddling. He was halfway across when thunder boomed above us. It startled Javier. He dropped one of his paddles in the water. Leaning over the edge, he tried to grab it. The canoe wobbled back and forth.

"Let it go!" I shouted. "You're going to fall out of the boat!"

I could only watch as Javier struggled to steady the canoe. I paced back and forth on the water's edge. I coaxed him forward. I knew he couldn't understand my words. But maybe the sound of my voice would steady him.

The rain was getting heavier. I worried it would fill his canoe.

He moved too slowly with one paddle. The flow of water began to pull him downriver.

He was only 30 feet away now. It might as well have been a hundred. I wanted to swim out and help him. But I remembered the warnings about whirlpools and drop-offs.

I could tell he was getting tired. The canoe kept drifting farther down the river. I sidestepped through the brush to keep up with him. Once, I tripped on a fallen limb and fell in the mud. I wiped my muddy hands on my jeans and kept going.

Javier was going to keep drifting if I didn't think of something. In a flash of lightning, I saw a fallen tree. It was hanging out over the river.

"There's a tree!" I shouted to Javier. "Paddle toward the tree!"

He had no idea what I was saying. I was so frustrated. If only I'd learned some Spanish. I needed that English-Spanish dictionary now! I tried to remember any word that might help.

"*Mirar!*" I screamed and pointed to the tree. "Look!"

Another flash of lightning lit up the dark sky. I saw him look at the tree. Then he started paddling with all his strength. He inched forward slowly.

"Grab the tree!" I yelled.

As the canoe drifted by, Javier grabbed a limb of the tree. The canoe rocked back and forth. In an instant, it flipped over. Javier was clinging to the branch.

I didn't even think about it. I just started climbing out on the tree. I worked my way through the branches. They were dead and dry, and they scraped my back. Some of them snapped under my weight. A couple of times, I almost fell through the branches into the river. But I kept going until I reached Javier.

I grabbed his arm and pulled him out of the water. Then we slowly worked our way back down the length of the tree. We reached the shore and let go of the tree. Relieved, we rolled onto the muddy ground.

We lay there in the rain taking in deep breaths. Once I had calmed down, I rolled over on one elbow to look at Javier. I could see his smile through the pouring rain.

"*Yo estoy en los Estados Unidos*," he said and grinned.

I didn't need a dictionary to understand those words.

"Yes." I smiled. "You're in the United States."

I was amazed that he would risk his life to come to the United States. I suddenly felt so proud to be an American.

Javier began to talk excitedly in Spanish.

"I don't know what you're saying," I said.

He continued to talk, swinging his arms around. All the while, he never quit smiling.

While he chattered, reality began to sink in. What was I going to do with him now? My first thought was Alfonso. Surely he would be willing to help Javier. If *he* couldn't help, I would have to tell Gramps.

Oh, no! Gramps! I had to get back to the barn right away. He was probably worried sick about me.

"Come on, Javier!" I said. I grabbed his arm and pulled him to his feet. "We have to get out of here."

I knew he didn't understand what I was saying. But he followed me through the brush anyway. As we walked, I tried to think about what I would tell Gramps. Maybe he wouldn't be mad when he saw Javier.

I was surprised how far we'd traveled downriver. We were at least a mile from the tractor. It was a long trek through the mud. After all of Gramps' stories, it felt creepy on the river after dark.

As we walked, I thought up excuses I could use to get myself out of trouble. I was concentrating so hard that I barely heard the muffled sound behind me. When I turned, I saw someone had grabbed Javier. Then a dark figure sprang out of the brush and grabbed me. A hand covered my mouth.

I struggled and fought to get free, but it was no use. The dark figures dragged us down into the brush.

Javier was really putting up a fight. Whoever had him pinned down was having a hard time. Javier kicked the man in the leg. I heard him moan in pain.

"*Silencio*," the man said to Javier. "*Yo no les voy hacer daño.*"

I didn't know what the man was saying. But Javier stopped struggling. The men uncovered our mouths. Javier didn't speak. I, however, had plenty to say.

"I don't understand Spanish!" I said in frustration. "I demand to know what's going on. Would you please speak in English?"

"He said to be quiet," one of the men whispered in English. "He said he wouldn't hurt you."

"Who are you?" I asked. "What do you want from us?"

"Are you American?" asked the man holding me. Before I could answer, he shined a flashlight in my face.

"Yes," I said. "And who are you?"

"I'm Sergeant Eduardo Soto with the U.S. Border Patrol," he said.

I could see the fallen look on Javier's face. He clearly understood the words *border patrol*.

"This is my partner, Joe Wilson," he said. He pointed to the other officer. "You two are interrupting our drug bust."

"What?" I asked in amazement.

"We got a tip," he said. "Three men are going to cross from the Mexican side tonight. We've been walking along the river searching for them."

I couldn't believe it! We had stumbled into a trap for drug traffickers!

Officer Soto explained the situation to Javier. His eyes were wide as he listened to the officer. Then Javier started rattling in Spanish. He was talking excitedly and pointing up the river.

The officers exchanged glances. "Do you think he knows what he's talking about?" Officer Soto asked the other officer.

"How do you know this boy?" Officer Wilson asked me.

I explained how I was helping my grandfather for the summer. I told them I had seen Javier sitting on the other side of the river. I explained how we had passed letters back and forth. And I admitted that he had just crossed the river.

"That matches his story," Officer Soto said, nodding at Javier. "He says he's seen the men we're talking about. He says they crossed about a half mile upriver."

"He watches the river every day," I told the officer. "I'm sure he knows what he's talking about."

"You boys will have to come along with us," said Officer Soto. "We can't leave you here alone."

Javier and I crouched down like the officers. We worked our way along the dark riverbank. The officer's flashlight put out very little light. The only other light was from the frequent lightning. I was thankful the rain had nearly stopped.

The officers used their radios to call for backup. They alerted the others to the new location.

As we neared the spot, Javier started whispering. He pointed to the other side of the river. The officers put on their night-vision goggles. They studied the riverbanks.

"The boy has good eyes," whispered Officer Soto. "There are three men at the edge of the water. It looks like they have three bundles. They're going to float them across."

I was amazed at what was happening around me. I felt as if I had suddenly entered a spy movie. I was hiding in the brush watching drug dealers. On one side of me were officers wearing night-vision goggles. On the other side was an illegal immigrant. I was scared but strangely excited too.

"Both of you stay right here," Officer Soto whispered. "I'm leaving one of the radios with you. But do not, under any circumstances, move from this spot."

"Yes, sir," I said. He didn't have to worry. I didn't *want* to move from that spot.

Javier and I watched the officers. They moved about ten yards down the river. Then they knelt in the grass, waiting.

We watched as the drug traffickers reached the American side. Each one had a bundle wrapped in plastic. They didn't make a sound as they pulled the bundles onto the shore.

Then the men slid the bundles into backpacks. They quietly slipped the packs over their shoulders and started to leave.

The backup still hadn't arrived. It looked as if the men would escape. The two officers had to make their move.

The officers jumped out of the brush and pointed their pistols at the men. Officer Soto shouted orders in Spanish. Immediately the men raised their hands in the air.

Officer Wilson yelled in Spanish. The men slid the backpacks off and dropped them on the ground. The officer kept his gun pointed at the men as he walked around to pick up their backpacks.

He ordered the three men to lie facedown on the ground. They put their hands behind their backs. Officer Wilson went around behind to handcuff them.

Two of the drug traffickers were quiet. But the other one started to argue.

Officer Wilson got behind him to handcuff him. As the officer reached down to grab his hands, the man flipped over. He caught Officer Wilson by surprise and pulled him to the ground.

Officer Soto held his gun on the other two men. Javier and I could only watch as Officer Wilson struggled with the third man.

Officer Wilson was strong, but he had a tough time. Then another captive began to argue with Officer Soto. Officer Soto shouted in return.

The officers seemed to be losing control. It was three against two. I remembered what Gran had said about drug traffickers. *They're dangerous. They'd do anything . . .*

I looked at Javier and whispered. "What are we going to do?"

He grabbed the radio and held it to my face. It was too dark to see the buttons on the radio. I was so desperate that I just held down different buttons and called for help. Finally I got a response.

"We need help!" I screamed into the radio. "Officer Soto and Officer Wilson have three drug—"

I never finished my sentence. A sound like a clap of thunder exploded into the dark, wet night. But I knew it wasn't thunder this time. It was a gunshot!

7
In Deep Trouble

Javier grabbed my arm. I dropped the radio in the mud.

We crouched down and peered through the brush. We wanted to stay hidden. But we also wanted to know what had happened. We could barely see the outlines of the men in the darkness.

Officer Soto had been knocked to the ground. His gun had gone off accidentally when he fell.

Officer Wilson was still wrestling with the same man. Officer Soto had to fight off the other two. Their hands were handcuffed behind their backs, but they were putting up quite a struggle.

One man started to run away, but Officer Soto tripped him. The man hit the ground hard and didn't get back up. The officer wrestled the other man to the ground. In just minutes, the officers had everything under control. *I* had a whole new respect for the border patrol.

Backup arrived just as the battle was over. The drug traffickers were led away in handcuffs. Javier and I watched Officer Soto examine the bundles. Officer Wilson was being checked out by a fellow officer.

"You have some nasty cuts," Officer Soto told him. "Why don't you ride in with Sergeant Perez? I'll take care of the boys."

"I think I'll do that," Officer Wilson said. "I'll see you at the station."

We walked with Officer Soto to his truck. Javier never made a sound. I could only imagine how disappointed he felt. He'd made all those plans to come to the United States. Now it looked as if he would be going right back to Mexico.

As for me, I was worried sick about what was going to happen next. I tried to swallow the lump in my throat. Then I asked the question.

"What are you going to do with us?" I asked.

"First I'm going to take you home," the officer answered.

"And what are you going to do with Javier?" I asked.

"I'll take him home too," he said. "To Mexico."

I looked at Javier. He didn't need to understand English. He knew what was happening.

"What's your name, son?" the officer asked me.

"Michael David Dawson III," I said.

"So you're Michael Dawson's grandson," he said.

"Yes, sir." I nodded. "Do you know my grandfather?"

"I've known Mr. Dawson for over 20 years," he said. "Sometimes we drink coffee together at El Taquito.

"I don't suppose your grandfather knows where you are, does he?" Officer Soto asked.

"No, sir," I said.

"Well, you two climb in," he said. "We'll go see what he has to say about it."

I wasn't looking forward to facing Gramps. He was going to be really upset. He had probably been worrying about me since sundown.

Javier still wasn't talking. I studied his face in the dashboard light. He was older than I'd thought. He might even be my age. His thick black hair was unevenly cut. He had coal-black eyes and dark brown skin.

He was soaking wet like me. And he was covered with mud from head to toe. He wasn't going to make a good first impression.

When we got home, all the lights were on. I glanced at the clock on the dashboard. It was midnight! Everyone was probably pacing the floor.

We walked to the front door. Javier and I looked terrible in the bright porch light. Gran hadn't complained about washing my greasy jeans. But I bet she was going to be mad this time.

Officer Soto rang the doorbell. I was so nervous, I felt sick. I dreaded seeing Gramps' face when he opened the door. He'd thought I was a responsible young man. I had really let him down.

I heard footsteps inside the house, and I braced myself. The door swung open. But it wasn't Gramps who answered the door. It was Dad!

He didn't even seem to notice the officer or Javier. He just looked right at me. At first I saw relief in his eyes. Then I saw anger.

"Michael!" he yelled. "Where in the world have you been?"

I was in worse trouble than I'd imagined. Gramps must have called Dad, and he'd flown in from Dallas. Before I could answer, the officer interrupted.

"Hey, Mike!" the officer said. "It's me, Eduardo Soto. I haven't seen you since we graduated."

"Eddie?" Dad asked in surprise. He stared at the officer and then at Javier. "What's going on?"

"You'd better step outside," the officer said. "You won't want these boys in the house."

Dad stepped outside and shut the door behind him.

"Where have you been, Michael?" Dad demanded. "You didn't come home on time, and Joe went looking for you. He said you and the tractor had disappeared. He's still out looking for you now."

Oh, no! Now I had Gramps, Dad, *and* Joe mad at me.

"I was with Javier at the river," I said.

"Who's Javier?" he asked.

"*This* is Javier," I said, pointing at him. "He's a friend of mine from Mexico."

"A friend from Mexico?" Dad asked.

I started at the beginning and told the whole story. I explained how we had communicated with letters. I told him how Javier had crossed the river. I was quick to tell him I'd tried to warn Javier not to try it. Then Officer Soto picked up the story from there.

"That's when we caught up with them," the officer said. "We were setting up a trap for a drug bust. The boys walked right into the middle."

"What?" Dad asked in disbelief.

"Turns out the drug traffickers were crossing somewhere else," the officer continued. "Javier helped us find them.

"We couldn't leave the boys alone on the river," he continued. "We had to take them with us. But we kept them at a safe distance. Thanks to Javier, we have the men in custody now."

Dad looked stunned. Then he turned and looked at me. "You're still in a lot of trouble, young man."

"Uh-huh," I agreed as I stared at the ground. "Is Gramps pretty mad too?"

"Your grandfather doesn't know anything about this," he said. "He's not home."

"Where is he?" I asked.

"He's in the hospital, Michael," Dad said. "He's had another heart attack."

8

A Temporary Pardon

"What?" I almost shouted.

Then I had a horrible thought. It was all my fault. He'd been so worried about me that he'd had another heart attack.

"Was it because of me, Dad?" I asked. I gulped and fought back the tears. "Was it because he was worried about me?"

"No, son," Dad said. He rested his hand on my shoulder to reassure me. "He had a heart attack about 4:30. We didn't know you were missing until after that. Joe and Grandma took him to the hospital. Then Joe went looking for you."

"But the doctor told Gramps that he was okay," I said.

"I guess the doctor was wrong," Dad said. "Grandma called and I took the first plane out of Dallas. We just got home from the hospital. I was about to go looking for you now."

"Is Gramps going to be all right?" I asked.

"I honestly don't know yet," Dad said slowly. "He's in intensive care. I can't see him again until tomorrow morning."

"I'm really sorry, Mike," Officer Soto said. "Your dad is a great guy."

"Thanks, Eddie," Dad said.

"At least Michael is home safely," the officer said. "And I'll make sure Javier gets back to Mexico."

"No!" I cried. "Please don't take Javier back! He wants to stay in the United States."

"That's Officer Soto's job," Dad said. "He has to take Javier back to Mexico. He crossed the border illegally."

"But, Dad," I pleaded. "You don't understand. He sits and stares across the river every day. He's been dreaming about coming here for a long time. He wants to go to school here and have a better life."

"I understand what you're saying," Dad said. "But there's nothing we can do for him."

"Just look at him, Dad," I said.

Javier looked pitiful. His clothes were still wet. He was covered in mud. But the look on his face said it all. He wanted to stay.

"What are you going to do with Javier?" Dad asked Officer Soto.

"He told me he has a brother named Ignacio," the officer replied. "He lives just across the border in Nuevo Progresso. I'll take him to the bridge. Then he can call his brother to come get him."

"He has a brother in Mexico?" Dad asked. "He must be worried about Javier."

"I asked Javier about that," the officer said. "He says he left a note for his brother. The note told him he was crossing tonight. Javier told him he would be safe. That he would be with a friend."

Dad took a long look at Javier again.

"Is it possible for you to leave him here tonight?" Dad asked. "I'll see to it that he gets back to Mexico tomorrow. At least he can get cleaned up and rest first."

"Normally I would never do that," the officer said, shaking his head. "But since it's you, I'll do it this time."

I breathed a sigh of relief and smiled at Javier. He smiled in return. Somehow he knew he was staying — at least for now.

"You guys go around to the back door," Dad said. "Leave your muddy clothes in a pile outside. I'll bring you some towels. Then go straight to the showers."

"Okay," I said.

"I'll let Gran know you're safe," said Dad. "She's tired and needs to go to bed."

"Come on, Javier," I said. I motioned for him to follow me. I was going to have to use a lot of hand motions. I really wished I had bothered to learn Spanish!

When we got inside, I led Javier to the downstairs bathroom. Javier's eyes opened wide. His mouth fell open. He stared at the inside of the house and mumbled in Spanish. It made me wonder what his house in Mexico looked like.

It took us a while to get rid of all the mud. Javier was grinning when he reappeared in a pair of my shorts and a T-shirt.

We were heading to the kitchen for a snack when we found Dad. He said Gran had gone to bed and he couldn't sleep. He made us some sandwiches and sat with us while we ate.

Javier quickly ate two sandwiches and half of a bag of potato chips. Then he took a deep breath and started on a third sandwich.

We heard a light knock on the back door.

"I asked Joe to come over," Dad said. "I knew you would want to apologize."

"Hi, Joe," I said. He looked tired and was wet and muddy too.

"Miguel," he said and nodded. I didn't get a hello or anything. It was obvious he was not happy with me.

"I'm really sorry you had to go out looking for me," I said. "I got so wrapped up with helping Javier. I just forgot about everyone else."

I was stumbling around with my apology. But I must have said something right.

Joe said, "Thinking about someone less fortunate than yourself is a good thing." He even smiled at me as he left.

It had been an exhausting day. When Javier finished eating, we headed to bed. I let Javier sleep in my bed. I slept in a sleeping bag on the floor next to him.

"Good night, Javier," I said as I turned out the lights.

"*Buenas noches*," he said.

When I awoke the next morning, Javier was still sleeping. I went to the kitchen looking for Dad. I found a note that said he and Gran had gone to the hospital. I set out the cereal and went back to wake up Javier.

Javier's Dream

As soon as he was awake, Javier started jabbering in Spanish. I just nodded as if I knew what he was saying.

It was impossible to make conversation over breakfast. So we just ate in silence. The language barrier was really bugging me.

After breakfast, I took Javier to the barn.

"Alfonso!" I called. "Are you in here?"

"Over here," he said. "I'm fixing a flat on a trailer."

"I want you to meet someone," I said, smiling. "Alfonso, meet Javier. Javier, meet Alfonso."

"Javier?" Alfonso said in surprise. "How did he get here?"

"It's kind of a long story," I said. I told him all about our adventures the night before.

Alfonso and Javier talked in Spanish and laughed.

"Stop!" I yelled. "I don't know what you're saying."

"Sorry," Alfonso said. "What do you want to know?"

"Ask about his family," I said.

Alfonso asked Javier the question. Then Alfonso interpreted the answer for me. Javier repeated what he'd said about his family in the letter.

"What about his father?" I asked.

I didn't know what Javier was saying, but I could tell he was upset.

"He says his father died last year," Alfonso said.

"I'm sorry," I said. I didn't know what else to say.

"Does he go to school?" I asked.

"Yes, he has finished the seventh grade," Alfonso said.

"He keeps staring at the house," I said. "Ask him what *his* house looks like."

I waited while Alfonso asked the question. Javier chattered in Spanish. His arms were waving around as he talked.

"He has a new house now," Alfonso said. "It's made with cement blocks and has a cement floor. The people from their church helped them build it.

"He says it's better than the house he was in before. It was made with mesquite limbs for the walls. The cracks between the limbs were filled in with cement."

"Oh," I said. Again, I didn't know what to say.

"He's also very proud that his family has electricity now," Alfonso added.

We continued to talk. I got a pretty good picture of Javier's life. It wasn't a very pretty picture.

9
A Painful Good-Bye

Javier had questions to ask too. He was surprised to learn that I lived in Dallas. He was *really* surprised that I didn't have any brothers or sisters. We were still talking when Gran and Dad returned.

"Gramps looks good," Gran said with a smile. "The doctor said he'll move to a regular room tomorrow. Then you can go see him."

"Great!" I said.

"Now it's time for us to get going," Dad said. "We need to take Javier back to Mexico."

"Hold on, Dad," I said. "I want to talk to you first."

He followed me out of the barn. I set lawn chairs in a shady spot under an ash tree. I wanted to make sure he was comfortable. That was always a good idea when I was about to ask for something big.

"Dad," I started. "I have an idea about Javier."

"I was afraid you might," Dad said.

"Let's take him back to Dallas with us," I said. "We have plenty of room at our house. He could live with us. He could go to school with me."

"Absolutely not!" Dad said. "There's no way we could do that."

"But why, Dad?" I asked.

"He's an illegal immigrant, Michael," he said. "Have you forgotten I promised Eddie that I'd return him to Mexico today? We can't take him to Dallas."

"But Gramps said it's legal to enter with a visa," I argued. "Couldn't we just get him a visa? We could pay for any fees."

"You don't understand the immigration process," he said. "You don't automatically get a visa just because you want one."

"But we could try," I insisted.

"Michael," Dad said patiently. "You don't even know this boy very well. Why do you feel so strongly about this?"

"He has so little, Dad," I pleaded. "And we have so much. I just want to help him."

"I think that's admirable," Dad said gently. "But we can't just move him into our home."

"So you're taking him back to Mexico?" I asked.

"Yes," he insisted.

"Can I go with you?" I whispered in defeat.

"If you wish," he said. "But remember, he will *not* be returning with us."

"Fine," I mumbled. I always knew when it was time to give up in an argument. There was a point when I knew Dad wasn't going to budge.

Dad asked Alfonso to drive us to Mexico. It was a short drive to the International Bridge and into Nuevo Progresso. From there, Javier directed us to the house he shared with his brother.

His home was in a row of similar structures. Many of them had no doors. It looked as if they had worn off their hinges years before.

"*Bienvenido*," Javier said as we entered the house.

"What did he say?" Dad asked.

"He said 'welcome,'" Alfonso explained.

I wasn't prepared for how bad his house would be. From the look on Dad's face, he wasn't either.

The whole house was one square room smaller

than my bedroom. The floor and walls were rough concrete. The roof was made of plywood. Sunlight shone in through the holes.

A mattress lay on the floor in one corner. A butane stove stood in another corner. A small, rusty refrigerator looked as if it hadn't kept anything cold in years. The only furniture was an old table with two chairs.

They didn't have many clothes. What they did have was neatly folded and stacked on the floor.

Dad was whispering to Alfonso. I heard him ask where the bathroom was.

"They share an outhouse with another family," Alfonso said.

I couldn't even look Javier in the eyes. It made me sick to think we were leaving him there.

Dad stumbled with his words. His normally cool exterior was gone.

"You're a very brave young man," Dad told Javier. "I hope you'll be able to come to the United States to live someday."

Javier never raised his eyes as Alfonso translated. "*Gracias*," he said softly.

There were so many things I wanted to say to him. But they were things I needed to say myself—not through an interpreter. I determined then that I was going to learn Spanish. I never wanted to be in a spot where I could not communicate again.

Alfonso explained that we could still write letters. He had Javier write down his address for me. I scribbled down my grandparents' address and our address in Dallas.

Javier finally raised his eyes and looked at me. "Gracias, Miguel," he said. "*Usted es un bien amigo.*"

"Good-bye, Javier," I said. "You're a good friend too."

Leaving Javier that day was the hardest thing I'd ever done. I wanted to scream at Dad for returning him to Mexico. I didn't, though, because it was easy to see that Dad was just as upset as I was.

10

A Dream Come True

Gran had dinner ready when we returned. All I did was push the food around on my plate. I wasn't interested in TV either. I finally gave up and went to bed. But every time I closed my eyes, I saw Javier in his house.

The next morning, I found Gran in the kitchen.

"Where's Dad?" I asked.

"He said he had some business to take care of," she replied.

"What kind of business?" I asked again.

"He didn't say," she said.

I thought it was strange, but I didn't really care. I was still worried about Javier.

"Would you like to go to the hospital with me?" Gran asked. "Joe said he would drive us."

"Yeah," I answered quickly. I needed to see for myself that Gramps was okay.

We found Gramps laughing with the nurses when we arrived. I figured that was a good sign he was going to be all right.

Dad had told him about Javier. He wasn't happy with me for keeping it from him. But he wasn't really mad either.

We visited Gramps for a couple of hours. When we returned home, Dad still wasn't there. Late that evening, he called and talked to Gran. He told her that his business wasn't finished and he'd be back later the next day. Finally, he asked about Gramps and then said good night.

It was after dinner the next day before he returned. He looked exhausted. His clothes were rumpled as if he'd slept in them.

"Where've you been?" I asked curiously.

"Let me sit down and I'll tell you," he said. He plopped down in a kitchen chair. "Could you get me something to drink?"

"Is everything all right?" I asked. "You look kind of worn-out."

"It's been a long couple of days," he said. He slipped off his shoes and propped up his feet. "I've spent the last two days with Mr. Falcon, an immigration lawyer."

"What?" I couldn't believe what I'd just heard. "Why were you with an immigration lawyer?"

"I couldn't get Javier off my mind the other night." He stopped to take a sip of his iced tea. "I finally got up and called your mother."

"Why did you call Mom?" I asked in confusion.

"I wanted to talk to her about Javier," he stated. "I explained the whole story—from how you met Javier to returning him to Mexico. I told her I wanted us to think about letting him come live with us."

"What?" I almost screamed. "What did she say? When is he coming? I can't believe it! I knew I could count on you!"

"Don't get too excited yet," Dad said. "I told you before that it's not that easy. There's a lot of red tape to unravel first."

"Red tape?" I questioned.

"A lot of steps to take. Rules to follow. It's not that easy," Dad said.

"At first I thought we could get him a student visa," Dad continued. "But student visas aren't issued to immigrants attending kindergarten though eighth grade.

"Then we looked at a visitor's visa. But that wouldn't work either. Those are for temporary visits for things like business or visiting relatives.

"Nothing would work for Javier. We almost gave up. Then Mr. Falcon came up with another plan."

"What?" I practically screamed. "What is it?"

"We could have Javier declared an orphan," Dad said. "Then we could adopt him."

"Are you saying he'd be my brother?" I asked in shock.

"Yes, son," he said with a smile. "He'd be your brother."

"Awesome!" I cried. "Unbelievably awesome!"

Gran heard me yelling and came running. I repeated the story to her. She seemed as shocked as I was.

"But Javier isn't an orphan," she pointed out. "He has a mother."

"Yes," Dad explained. "But there's a section in the law that says if his remaining parent can't care for him properly, he can be declared an orphan. However, the parent has to sign a document allowing the adoption."

"Do you think she'll do that?" Gran asked.

"I know she will," Dad said confidently. "We talked with her today."

"Huh?" I said in surprise.

"Mr. Falcon and I talked to Javier's brother at work. We explained the situation to him. We asked him what their mother would think of such an idea.

"Ignacio said he wasn't sure what his mother would do. But he also said he knew how much it meant to Javier. He told us he would talk to her.

"He called his mother and explained our plan. She wanted to see Javier first before she would make a decision. So we took Javier to Veracruz to see his mother."

"No way!" I said.

"We talked through an interpreter. Javier told her how important it was to him to find a better life. I told her about all the opportunities he would have in America.

"Javier also made it clear that he was proud of his Mexican heritage. He told her that he loved his family and was proud of them. He said he would stay in touch with them and go for regular visits. Someday he hopes to be able to send them money so they can have a better life too."

"So what did she say?" I pressed.

"I think it was hard for her," his dad said, "but she finally agreed. She signed the necessary papers."

"So where is he?" I asked excitedly. I glanced around the room, expecting him to appear.

"No, son," he said. "That's just the first step. Next, your mother and I have to sign some papers. Then we have to be approved as adoptive parents. Once that's done, the adoption will be final and Javier will be an American citizen."

I wished I had been there to see Javier's face. He must have been thrilled when he heard he would soon become an American citizen.

"So what do we do now? How long will all this take?" I asked. The sooner Javier could get here, the better.

"I thought we would fly home after Gramps gets home from the hospital. I want your mother to sign the papers as soon as possible. After that, we'll see."

"But I don't want to go home yet," I said.

Now it was Dad's turn to look surprised.

"You don't?" he asked. "What about baseball camp?"

"It's not for a couple more weeks," I replied. "I want to stay here until camp starts."

"Can I ask why?" he questioned me.

"We're going to have to wait a few days for the ground to dry out," I explained. "Then there are more cotton stalks to be shredded."

"You sound just like your grandfather," Dad said with a smile.

I knew Dad didn't care much for farming. But over the past few weeks, I'd realized how much I liked it. Gramps said he had farming in his blood. Maybe I'd inherited that blood.

"I guess it will be all right if you stay two more weeks," Dad agreed.

"Thanks, Dad," I said and relaxed for the first time in days.

Gramps came home a few days later. Dad flew home as scheduled.

After the fields dried out, I went back to work shredding cotton stalks. Joe and Fausto followed behind me, plowing up the remainder of the stalks.

When it was time for baseball camp, it was hard to leave. I was really going to miss everyone.

"Thanks for helping out," Gramps said. He handed me my paycheck and patted me on the back. "You're welcome to come back anytime."

"I was thinking maybe next summer," I said. "If you get some good rains in the spring, you could have a bumper crop next summer."

He was obviously pleased at my interest in the farm. He got so choked up that he couldn't talk.

"That would be great," Gran said proudly. "We'll be looking forward to it."

I was happy to get back home but sad at the same time. I had hoped that Javier would be returning with me.

Dad assured me he was still working on the adoption. He reminded me that the process for immigration and adoption was long and complicated. Javier and I would just have to wait a while longer.

Baseball camp went well. I was picked as one of the pitchers for the tournament on the last day. I even struck out four batters.

When camp was over, it was time for school to start. I hated that Javier wasn't there to begin with me.

At least we kept in touch. I received a letter from him each week. His brother helped him with it. I wrote him about the news at school. I thought going to school in Texas might seem scary to him. So I explained how the class schedule worked. I also told him all about the teachers.

He was hoping to arrive before Halloween. I'd told him about the costume party that Grady always had. During the party, everyone went to a local haunted house and scared one another.

But the adoption process still wasn't final by then.

I was really disappointed when he didn't arrive in time for Thanksgiving. Dad let me carve the turkey for the first time. It was quite an honor. But I couldn't help thinking about Javier all day. He would have loved that big Thanksgiving dinner.

By December, Javier and I were both frustrated. We didn't even mention being together for Christmas. We didn't want to be let down again.

My family went all out on decorations. Dad and I put up twice as many lights as usual. Our Christmas tree was huge. We could barely fit it in the house. We put presents for Javier under the tree, although we never spoke about him being with us for the holiday.

About a week before Christmas, Dad went out of town on a last minute business trip. Mom stayed busy with her holiday baking. I didn't have anything to do. Waiting around for good news drove me crazy.

I was glad when Grady invited me to a movie. It didn't even matter that I'd seen the show before. I just wanted to get out of the house.

Javier's Dream

Afterward we stopped for pizza. Then we headed to Grady's house for some video games. It was late when I got home.

I heard Dad's voice when I opened the front door. I didn't realize he'd be back so soon. I followed the sound of his laughter into the kitchen.

At first I didn't notice the extra person sitting at the kitchen table. Then it hit me.

"Javier!"

"*Buenos dias*," he replied, grinning.

For a second I didn't know what to say. Then everything poured out.

"I was hoping you'd be here for Christmas. It wouldn't have been the same without you. You'll love my mom's cookies. We bought lots of presents for you . . ."

I realized I was jabbering. Javier probably couldn't understand a word. But I was so excited that I couldn't help myself.

I grabbed his arm and pulled him through the house.

"We have a great Christmas tree," I said. "Have you seen it yet?"

I didn't let him answer as I pulled him up the stairs.

"I want to show you our room. We bought you a bunch of baseball stuff. I didn't know if you like other sports. Grady and I like basketball and soccer too—"

"Miguel," he interrupted me.

"Yes?" I said, stopping to look at him.

"Yo estoy en los Estados Unidos," he whispered.

"Yes," I said. "You're in the United States. And this time you're here to stay."

Javier's dream had finally come true.